Dear Parent:
Your child's love of reading s

Every child learns to read in a different way and at his or her own speed. You can help your young reader improve and become more confident by encouraging his or her own interests and abilities. You can also guide your child's spiritual development by reading stories with biblical values and Bible stories, like I Can Read! books published by Zonderkidz. From books your child reads with you to the first books he or she reads alone, there are I Can Read! books for every stage of reading:

SHARED READING
Basic language, word repetition, and whimsical illustrations, ideal for sharing with your emergent reader.

BEGINNING READING
Short sentences, familiar words, and simple concepts for children eager to read on their own.

READING WITH HELP
Engaging stories, longer sentences, and language play for developing readers.

READING ALONE
Complex plots, challenging vocabulary, and high-interest topics for the independent reader.

ADVANCED READING
Short paragraphs, chapters, and exciting themes for the perfect bridge to chapter books.

I Can Read! books have introduced children to the joy of reading since 1957. Featuring award-winning authors and illustrators and a fabulous cast of beloved characters, I Can Read! books set the standard for beginning readers.

A lifetime of discovery begins with the magical words **"I Can Read!"**

Visit www.icanread.com for information on enriching your child's reading experience.
Visit www.zonderkidz.com for more Zonderkidz I Can Read! titles.

Always try to be kind to each other
and to everyone else.
—1 Thessalonians 5:15

ZONDERKIDZ

Frank and Beans and the Grouchy Neighbor
Copyright © 2010 by Kathy-jo Wargin
Illustrations © 2010 by Anthony Lewis

Requests for information should be addressed to:

Zondervan, *Grand Rapids, Michigan 49530*

Library of Congress Cataloging-in-Publication Data

Wargin, Kathy-jo.
    Frank and Beans and the grouchy neighbor / story by Kathy-jo Wargin ;
pictures by Anthony Lewis.
       p. cm.
    Summary: When their grouchy neighbor joins Frank, his parents, and Beans
on a fishing trip, things go from bad to worse, until Frank realizes the cause
of his neighbor's unfriendliness.
    ISBN 978-0-310-71849-9 (softcover)
    [1. Loneliness—Fiction. 2. Fishing—Fiction. 3. Dogs—Fiction. 4. Christian life—
Fiction.] I. Lewis, Anthony, 1966- ill. II. Title.
PZ7.W234Fp 2010
[E]—dc22
{B}   2009003011

Scriptures taken from the Holy Bible, *New International Reader's Version®, NIrV®.* Copyright © 1995, 1996, 1998 by Biblica, Inc.™ Used by permission of Zondervan. All rights
reserved worldwide.

Any Internet addresses (websites, blogs, etc.) and telephone numbers printed in this book
are offered as a resource. They are not intended in any way to be or imply an endorsement
by Zondervan, nor does Zondervan vouch for the content of these sites and numbers for the
life of this book.

Zonderkidz is a trademark of Zondervan.

Editor: *Mary Hassinger*
Art direction: *Jody Langley*

Printed in China

10 11 12 13 14 15 /SCC/ 6 5 4 3 2 1

Frank and Beans
and the
Grouchy Neighbor

story by Kathy-jo Wargin

pictures by Anthony Lewis

Frank waved goodbye

to Birdie and Grandma.

He put on his fishing vest.

Frank walked to the car.

"Let's go, Beans. Let's go to the lake."

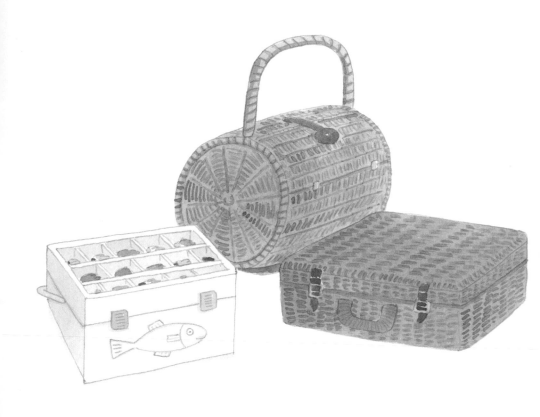

"We have bait and baskets of food,"
said Frank's dad.

"Let's hope we don't get them mixed up!"
said Frank's mom, grinning.

Frank rolled down the window.

The wind felt nice.

Beans' ears flapped in the wind.

The day could not get better.

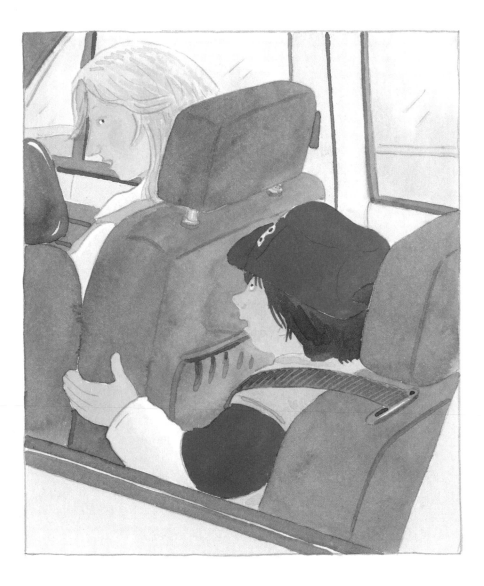

"Why are we stopping?" Frank asked.

Before Mom could answer,

Mr. Granger appeared.

He had a fishing pole and a bag.

Mr. Granger lived alone.

Mr. Granger was grumpy sometimes.

He did not like dogs.

Frank gave his mom a sour look.

"Frank," she said,

"Mr. Granger is old.

He spends too much time alone.

God wants us to care for others.

That means sharing our time."

Frank pouted.

Beans pouted too.

Mr. Granger climbed into the car.

"I brought cookies," he said.

Then he looked back at Beans.

"I hope that dog will behave today!"

Mr. Granger said.

15

They got to the lake.

"Where are my cookies?"

asked Mr. Granger.

Beans was sitting by an empty bag.

His nose was covered in crumbs.

"Dogs are big trouble,"

said Mr. Granger.

In the boat, Mr. Granger was quiet.

He watched his bobber.

Then his pole moved!

"I think you have a big one," said Dad.

"Hooray!" shouted Mom.

Everyone was happy.

Mr. Granger smiled too.

Frank grabbed the net to help.

Beans wanted to help too.

Beans got very close to Frank.

He knocked the net from Frank's hand.

The fish was lost.

Mr. Granger said,

"I told you dogs were big trouble."

Frank wanted to go home.

He was happy to go to shore.

Mr. Granger was on the dock.

Beans stepped on his foot.

SPLASH!

Mr. Granger fell into the lake.

Mr. Granger said to Beans,

"Look what you have done.

I am soaking wet!"

Beans felt sorry.

He leaned over to kiss Mr. Granger.

SPLASH!

Beans was in the lake too.

Frank jumped in to save Beans.

Now all three were in the lake!

Mr. Granger started to laugh.

"I am sorry, Frank,"

said Mr. Granger.

"I have not been very nice.

Feeling lonely makes me grouchy."

Frank said, "That's okay.

God wants us to care about others

even when we do not feel like it.

I was grouchy too. I am sorry too!"

Mr. Granger laughed again.

He said, "God wants us to forgive.

I forgive you."

"Do you forgive Beans too?"

Frank pointed at Beans.

"Yes, I forgive Beans too."

"Next stop, Cooper's Diner,"
said Frank's dad.
"I hear they have tasty fish."

Mr. Granger shared his fish

with his new best friend, Beans.

Beans enjoyed every bite!